The Devil's In The Cows

Flash fiction by

Sippican Cottage

P.O. Box 81226
Seattle, WA 98108
USA
www.createspace.com

Portions of this book previously appeared at
www.sippicancottage.blogspot.com
Illustrations are from the Library of Congress and are in the public
domain

Loke, fahter: your sone!

Contents

All you need is ignorance and confidence and the success is sure.

-Mark Twain

I don't care if people think you write like Mark Twain, or Shania Twain. Publish it.

-My wife

The Devil's In The Cows

The Devil's In The Cows

I TOLD THAT boy, I told him. You don't want no part of this farm, nor another. A farm is a jackplane for human boards. Wears you out like a sermon.

It made *ma mere* old, and his mother, too. She was beautiful once. Gone to seed, now. The work wore at her. Not the work, no -- getting nothing for the effort but chapped grinds a person down. A farm is a twenty-five hour timeclock with no paycheck. She done it for me, and I done it for the farm, and for *pere* and *ma mere*, but it dies with me.

It's a terrible thing to raise your own to disown you. The girls was no trouble 'cause all girls like frilly things and a farm is a dreary place. First magazine comes into a farmhouse with pictures of socialites, and daughters is plotting an escape. The only mistake they can make is letting some local boy convince them that he's the ticket out of here. A wandering mind and a weak back is fine for a city dweller, but it's deadly out in the landscape. The farmboys with a touch of neon about them and their coquettes generally break down and wander back before they even get to a road with two stripes on it. We sent the girls to Augusta to school, and they found fellers with ink daubed all over them and we breathed a sigh.

"It's a boy!" my wife said, "We were blessed with a boy, Xavier, and he can help you." But I already knew in my heart that it was a curse, because I loved that boy so, before he was even borned, that I could never let him like me much.

He had to see how hard life was here and so put aside a man's sneaky love for his father and go away someday.

I had to goad him from this place. That is a hard thing, my friend -- a hard thing.

My father in his turn told me all of the things a man needs to know about a farm, in his mind, anyway. He loved it so, and tried to make me love it too. I loved him, truth be told, but hated his farm. But he got rheumy and I stayed on to help and eventually I slipped him in the ground and threw dirt on him like any other seed. By then it was too late to slip the orbit.

So I shows my boy what's what, and drive him like a team from dawn to dusk his whole life. I gotta wear it out of him early. He learned everything about the old place, but it's all bad son, all bad, I says over and over. He'd keep even with me when he was only shoulder height, and I'd catch him sneaking a bed lunch for the power that was in it. I didn't know what to do with him after a while, to discourage him, for I could never bring myself to be mean with him -- never.

Then the boy comes to me and says there's a war on, father, and I'm gonna go and kill a *Boche* or two. And my wish is granted and I curse the genie like all men do that go for a rub expecting a free lunch.

The kids from the city will think it's a lark until they're pissing themselves in a trench, and could no more kill anyone than a kitten. That's good, and might keep them safe. But the boy's never been afraid like that, and that's bad.

"You remember *gran-pere*, boy?"

"Of course, dad."

"Well, I've never been no more good to you than a Pharaoh to a Jew, but now you have to listen to me.

Gran-pere he was wise about the world. It wasn't about knowing things; any damn fool knows things, some of them true. *Gran-pere* could feel things. He went beyond the knowing and let himself *feel* things. You got to do that. It's in you, I know it, because he drew it out of me, and you're mine."

"I feel things, dad."

"No, not like that. Not moonin' over the neighbor's girl or getting angry over the radio. It's sense -- like smell or something. It's not on purpose. *Laissez faire*, boy."

"Dad, the train is leaving."

"I remember when I was young and we was working, *gran-pere* would put his nose up in the air and mutter, "The devil's in the cows." The sky might be dead blue, not a puff of wind, six hours of work to be done, and we'd go inside; within an hour the heavens would open up and we'd watch weather as stupefying as any ten pages of the Bible from the parlor."

"Goodbye, dad."

I saw him sit, the familiar shrug of his blocky shoulders clear as day through the glass, and then the train slowly pulled away. He didn't look back.

Oh God -- watch for the devil in the cows, son.

So What

I WOULDN'T PUT my finger in that change return slot if there was fifty bucks in it. The greasy handset, battered by a numberless army of salesmen and lovers, hangs like a murderer on a gibbet over the thing. Let the bums get it. She said she'd come. I'm not calling her anymore.

I loved the feeling of the neon glowing on the side of my face in the lobby. Don't tell me it's just light. I feel it like the sun. It's the only sun I'll ever acknowledge. The one in the morning rises alone. Mine rises when the manager flips the switch. It never sets on me, that sun.

Man, that scirocco of sweat and booze and cigs and breath like a welder's tank. I feel like I'm born again, from a mummy's womb. Straight on in, just like the music.

The stage is exactly three inches higher but a galaxy away from the dance floor. Dance floor? Please. Stumble around with a woman that ain't your wife floor, I think. I like the old dude that looks like Batman's butler or a fruity sort of baron or something that conducts or sways or whatever it is he's doing. He's possessed with it, same as me. He's usually possessed of plenty of cake, a desire to buy a man a drink, and an aversion to arithmetic, too. The waitresses adore that.

The curtain is dirty from wiping your hands on it. Me included. It's dirty like life is. Up high, it's dirty with cobwebs and dust and corruption because you can't reach up there. Down low it's dirty with the grubby hands of all of us trying to wipe off the sweat and grease of what you're doing.

I listen for the cornshucks of the brushes on the snare.

He hits it, but I don't care about that. In between -- the faint circular sketching he does without thinking -- that's what I'm after. He's lathering the dry face of the song so I can shave it with the sharp edge of the brass. The bass rumbles like thunder in the distance.

I can taste metal and blood and booze in my mouth. Tastes like life.

Hope Street

"CAN YOU TELL ME the way to Hope Street?"

"They tell me the road to hope is long, and fraught with peril, sir."

(*Stunned silence. A moment of recognition. Wry smile.*)

"Yes, officer, but at least it's paved now."

"The cobbles are made from the hearts of damp policemen, sir. They are only mortared loosely with good intentions."

"You have the gun, so I defer to your judgment. The way?"

"Go back up the hill and turn right, if you want to find Hope. Abandon hope, all ye who stand here in the middle of the street with a policeman in the sleet."

"Would you like a cup of coffee, officer?"

"What I would *like* is a gold-plated Republican job and a roast turkey with a side order of another roast turkey, and a whiskey and an upholstered woman with a fireplace and access to more whiskey, thank you. But I'll *settle* for a cup of coffee, if that's what you meant."

"I'll need to cross the street to get it. Will you stop the traffic?"

"Sir, I'll hold them here until the ammo runs out, then go hand to hand with the stragglers, if you'll bring a sinker with the joe."

"Done, and done."

"Are those your lawyers, sir?"

"Spring is coming, officer, if we keep this up."

"Go! I'll cover you."

Ginger Ale

I WISH IT WOULD rain. No. Sleet. Sleet would finish the scene nicely. Rain is God's mop. It washes away the dirt and corruption. I've got no use for snow, either; the fat flakes are too jolly. Snow makes a fire hydrant into a wedding cake. I want sleet.

I'd rather pull my collar up and hunch my shoulders as if blows from an unseen and merciless boxer were raining down on me. I don't want a Christmas card. I want the Old Testament.

Old or new - I knew it. Father and mother would open the Bible to a random page and place an unseeing finger anywhere and use it for their answer to whatever question was at hand. They'd torture the found scripture to fit the problem a lot, but it was uncanny how often that old musty book would burp out something at least fit for a double-take. But any Ouija board does that, doesn't it?

It was just cold and bracing. No sleet. I didn't need to be clear-minded right now. Paul's tip of the hat to the season, a sort of syphilitic looking tree, hung over your head as you entered the bar like it was Damocle's birthday, not the Redeemer's. It was kinda funny to see it out there, because inside it was always the same day and always the same time. Open is a time.

People yield without thinking in these situations. It had been years since I had found anyone sitting on that stool, my place. It was just understood, like the needle in the compass always pointing the same way for everyone. Paul never even greeted me anymore, just put it wordlessly down in front of me as I hit the seat. Some men understand other men.

It was already kind of late. My foreman said for all he cared, I could bang on those machines until Satan showed up in the Ice Capades, but I didn't feel like working on Christmas Eve until the clock struck midnight. That's a bad time to be alone and sober.

"I'm closing early tonight," Paul said, and he didn't go back to his paper or his taps. He just stood there eying me. I took the drink.

"You've made a mess of this, Paul," I stammered out, coughing a bit, "What the hell is this?"

"It's ginger ale. You're coming with me tonight."

I could see it all rolled out in front of me. Pity. Kindness. Friendship.

"No." I rose to leave.

"You'll come, or you'll never darken the doorstep here again."

Now a man finds himself in these spots from time to time. There are altogether too many kind souls in the world. They think they understand you. They want to help you. But what Paul will never understand is that he was helping me by taking my money and filling the glass and minding his own. It was the only help there was. A man standing in the broken shards of his life doesn't have any use for people picking up each piece and wondering aloud if this bit wasn't so bad. They never understand that the whole thing was worth something once but the pieces are nothing and you can never reassemble them again into anything.

I went. Worse than I imagined, really. Wife. Kids. Home. Happy. I sat in the corner chair, rock-hard sober, and then masticated like a farm animal at the table.

Paul was smarter, perhaps, than I gave him credit for. He said nothing to me, or about me. His children nattered and his wife placed the food in front of me and they talked of everything and nothing as if I wasn't there – no, as if I had always been there. As if the man with every bit of his life written right on his face had always sat in that seat.

I wasn't prepared for it when he took out the Bible. Is he a madman like my own father was? It's too much. The children sat by the tree, and he opened the Bible and placed his finger in there. I wanted to run screaming into the street. I wanted to murder them all and wait for the police. I wanted to lay down on the carpet and die.

"Ye are the salt of the earth; but if the salt have lost his savour, wherewith shall it be salted? It is thenceforth good for nothing, but to be cast out, and to be trodden under foot of men. Ye are the light of the world. A city that is set on an hill cannot be hid. Neither do men light a candle, and put it under a bushel, but on a candlestick, and it giveth light unto all that are in the house. Let your light so shine before men, that they may see your good works, and glorify your Father which is in heaven."

He put the children to bed, to dream of the morning. His wife kissed him, said only "good night" to me, and went upstairs. We sat for a long moment by the fire, the soft gentle sucking sound of the logs being consumed audible now that the children were gone. The fire was reflected in the ornaments on the tree. The mantel clock banged through the seconds.

"Do you want something?" he asked.

"Ginger ale."

27

It All Just Was

DELIGHTFUL TO COME to Truro. Never in high season. When the winter's done pounding the sand as flat and hard as concrete, every footprint erased -- that's the time to come.

The light is captivating in the early spring. The dish of the sun hangs low in the southern sky, even at noon, and reaches into the room to pick out the details of the most mundane of objects. The owners keep such a treasure trove of trash in here. There's a weird vibe to a room filled with things that aren't important enough to throw away. They are like amulets on the fritz, unable to ward off evil, just the cleaning lady now. Shims under the bockety leg of someone else's life. Like finding a totem in the wilderness from a dead tribe. It's the lost-and-found in an abandoned asylum.

The first few times I stayed here, I'd pick up one awful thing after another and wonder: what could possibly make someone bring this into the house, never mind keep it through all these years? What power did these talismans hold for their owners? Why build an altar of peeling paint and mildewed wallpaper to worship this god of kitsch?

I got over it. I'd hear the scree of the spring and the slap of the screen door behind me and wander the sand alone, trying to impartially divide my hearing between the whistle of the wind, the sigh of the surf, and the shh shh of the dune grass reminding me I was in their nursery.

There was no point to the things in the shack, or the lapping of the idiot ocean against the fool earth.

In the pale moonlight it all went about its business whether I was awake or not. It all just was.

I'd call the people and tell them I wanted to stay in the cottage where it all just was, and they'd put their hand over the receiver for a moment and I knew they were using the word "daft" to their companion about that fellow that wanted to go where no one wanted to go in a season when no one went anyway. Then they'd come back and say they had checked and there looked to be a hole in the schedule. There's a hole in Hiroshima, too, I'd think, but not say.

I've always liked the little stove. You sit right next to it and feed it like a baby. You can put your hands right on the cool metal after you light a fire in it, and feel the power of the flames slowly mount to warm your hands. It gets too hot in an instant, like so many things.

You can feed a stove almost anything on a cold morning. Kindling. Rags. A love letter.

Holding It Back

IT'S A SOLITARY THING, to write. I hole myself up in a place that's illegal to put a murderer in -- too small; but you have to get away from the wrong kind of noise. Cicadas are OK. The wheezing of the refrigerator cycling on and off is not. A lawnmower four blocks away is delightful. Next door makes you dream of slitting throats.

My wife looks after the workmen. All their noise, and every other aspect they exhibit to the world, is foul. They get up too early and still smell of last night's revelry. They swear loudly as their feet crunch noisily in the gravel of the driveway, thinking that by some magical transubstantiation of time and space they're not brutes if they only swear outside where the woman isn't. They remind me of a pack of dogs, only not as clean.

All save one. I watch him. I can't write while they're knocking around the place, so I started to watch out of boredom and frustration. There is one guy...

I don't know how to explain it, though explaining things is my business. No, that's not right. I obfuscate and fill the pages. I do describe, though. How to describe him?

He's not like the others; it's the best I can do. I made a serious error once, and they noticed me looking and started talking to me. The fetid gravy of my money being wasted was basted over the banal lump of their interests. I retreated. I watched from afar.

You didn't need to be close to see he was different. He never spoke but to make himself understood. He pointed to things with his index finger, but never pointed to a person that way. I wonder if anyone but me ever noticed

33

that. The beasts that were his brethren never noticed anything except noontime.

He seemed to be in charge in a way I've never seen. Maybe in the military it's that way, when the green lieutenant is getting everyone killed, including himself eventually, and the older and savvier sergeant starts to point the way inferentially. The ideas must not seem to come from you, just appear in the ether.

He was not in charge in name. He was one of them. The fellow in charge was never there except to apply verbal emollients to my wife and extract a payment from me. But when he left, they all looked to the quiet man.

How did he do it? I couldn't look straight at these buggers to divine it; but even if I could, I don't think I would be able to get the hang of it just by figuring it out. People yammer in team-building exercises in conference rooms all the time about leading by example, but they are like teenage boys talking about grown women. It's academic what you'd do.

I became obsessed with the idea. Why did this fellow command others' respect? Not fear, or affection, not even interest -- respect. Why did they defer to his judgment without even knowing it? Who taught this man? Is it on a shelf somewhere, a plebeian Eliot's five-foot shelf of books?

The others always left five minutes early. He'd poke around their work, usually dropped wherever it stood, and move it a bit so it wouldn't fall over. He'd turn their plane irons on their side while using the side of his boot to coax the little cut-off blocks scattered everywhere away from underfoot.

It was like watching a calloused Jeeves tidying an absent Wooster's room without seeming to expend any effort. Extraordinary.

"Good afternoon," I said.

"Yes, it's certainly that."

"I've been watching you."

"You have paid the band. It's your tune."

"You have a way about, you; it's interesting."

"Everyone..."

There was a certain kind of a pause. I'd picked up on it. An insuck of breath, almost inaudible. A kind of weariness? I don't know.

"Everyone has a way about them, sir."

"My name is David. Call me David, please."

"Yes, sir."

"I wanted to ask you how..." I hesitated just there.

"Yes?"

"How it is you do it."

"Do what, sir?"

"What you do; I'm not sure how to encompass the whole question in one question. The others, they look to you for what to do. They watch you all the time and you bend them to your will."

"I do nothing of the sort, sir."

"I've watched you. You might not know it, but you do."

There was another slight insuck of air. I didn't know what to expect. I shouldn't have confronted him, perhaps, but I had to get this on paper or the whole month was a loss. My wife would have her house and I'd have nothing but a pile of blank foolscap and a ravished bank account. I could get something out of this guy. He was interesting.

He seemed to unstick himself, and asked me, "Do you know *Lawrence of Arabia*, sir, when Lawrence is shot at the train, and the reporter takes Auda's picture?"

"You mean the movie? No, we don't go to movies. I read the *Seven Pillars of Wisdom* in school.

There was another little chuff of breath.

"Do you know Elvin Jones, sir?"

"The drummer?"

"Yes, that's him."

"What's he got to do with Lawrence of Arabia?"

"Nothing, sir, I expect. But it's like him."

"I don't follow you. You're a musician, too?"

"I am not. But you see, when Elvin Jones is playing the ride cymbal. Do you know it?"

"I must admit I don't follow you."

"You see, it just sizzles. It sizzles with a kind of power."

"But it's quiet. He just touches it."

"No. Don't you understand, he's bringing his arm down, every time, as hard as he can -- and at the same time, he's holding it back, holding it back, but not quite as hard as he's hitting it, and the leftover hits the cymbal."

"I must say, I don't mean to be rude, but you talk in circles, sometimes."

Then he took his hammer out of his toolbelt and plunged it three inches deep into the plaster wall, an inch from my head.

"Got it?"

They Run And Hide Their Heads

I **REMEMBER THE WAY** it used to drum on the corrugated roof.

Rain in the city is nothing. I love the sound of it still, but the whole place, from the scuppers in the parapet walls above down to the pipes below the street, are only there to make it go away. It scours the street and washes away the children's chalk on the sidewalks and makes its lonely way to the sea, but it doesn't feed anything here.

I remember my father. He'd stand in his field, lean on one ash handle or another – all bought rough and made smooth with his uncountable exertions-- take off his hat, wipe his brow, and scan the skies for a long moment. I'd watch him and wonder what might rumble through a head such as his. If he spoke ten thousand words in his lifetime, I'd be surprised to hear it. I never heard them.

He was watching for rain, of course. A man with fingers of green just coming out of his rows keeps his eye on the horizon. It's not a matter of forgetting an umbrella and having to hustle from the trolley to the vestibule. It's life and death.

"Be careful what you wish for," was one of the few things my father did say. He'd say it whenever anybody said something stupid at the Grange Hall. "There's no free lunch," would usually follow. Father knew about a sword with two edges. Everything has two edges on a farm.

And so he would scan the skies with that squint of his, born of countless days under that forbidding sun, and pray for sweet, precious rain.

He knew that if it did not come, we were done for, and those tender shoots would stand like dun headstones in his field. But he also knew that the thing he fervently prayed for might wash us all away in a maelstrom. It is an odd thing, to earnestly pray for the thing that might save you, but that could just as easily crush you like the bugs we all are. But that's what any prayer is, isn't it?

Father and the farm are both gone now. I reach out from under the porch eave and let the drops hit my hand before the city throws them all away.

Jupiter And Mars

THAT KID HE BOMBS around the lot in my Caddie and I've got my heart in my throat just tossing him the keys but he never misses so what the hell. He's dressed like he's waiting for an organ grinder, but the missus think's he's some kinda handsome and what's the harm in that. Young man should be handsome and see some hubba-hubba wife now and then so he knows why-for he's groping that neighborhood girl in the back of a jalopy.

Jesus she steps out like a queen. The monkey missing his tin cup holds the door and she puts out one leg with the seam running up the back and he's transfixed like a gimp at Lourdes and she's coming down from a cloud. She's got a halo of perfume and a cloud of radiation from the neon sign on her silk and glitters a bit on the fingers. We go in and the Caddie gets its workout.

There's the maitre d and he knows me and there's no fuss except the fussing over a guy likes. The wife inspects the drop ceiling like it's a chapel while Rocco says his little prayer of a tip and massages me a bit. He inspects the long-memorized seating plan like it's a lost scroll instead of his reason for being. "I might just have something near the floor 'cause I know missus, well, she can dance is what I'm sayin'."

The coat check girl is the homely one, and even she could start a knifefight on any corner in Naples just by walking past. The girl who takes you to the table could get the Pope to reconsider.

There's too many onions but they're sweet. The wood pressed into a little quilt reveals itself as you make your way to the bottom of the bowl.

Bread in a basket, O and V in the cruets, two ashtrays. Chianti, Franco; ten bucks and it's the best chianti in the world, with the cock right there on the stripe like back home. The stuffy guys, the dentists with Yankee names come in here and order *sangiovese* for their stringy wives to ooh and aah over and pay twenty 'cause they don't know no better.

The dentist Yankees drift by on the dance floor and you can see them eying the real woman you got, pushing the limits of her dress every which place -- Bam! Boop! Bap! -- and he's got the skinny sorority girl who moves around like a giraffe in a straightjacket and you know right off that she moves like that everywhere. That's why he can't stop robbing a peek at the missus when he can; they always sneak out of the house in their mind in here, the white bread. They couldn't handle a woman like I got anyway. They should stick to the ingenues who reach for the diazepam instead of the kitchen knives when you piss them off.

In other words, please be true. In other words, I love you.

A Life Full Of Nothing

THIS IS ALL there is of him now.

Oh how he railed about bankers. Mother would remind him, occasionally, that he was a banker. He'd splutter and rage and Mother would leave to see what the cook was doing and return and neither of them ever missed a beat. I'd watch the dirty urban raindrops wend their way down the panes, backlit by the milky sunshine that was our ration at the end of the brownstone canyon, and pray for it all to end. The rain, the impotent rage, all of it. Now it's done.

I wander through the empty rooms, all full of nothing, but then again, they always were. I never heard it put better than that. A life full of nothing. There was always someplace to be; something that required his immediate attention; something innocuous that would bring on the stemwinding peroration, to no one in particular, about the hard, cold heart of everyone who dared come into his line of sight when he was trying to make the column on the left and the column on the right match up. A life devoted to those damn dots.

I never could muster any awe or fear of the old man. He was volcanic, and yet the rumblings signified nothing. The threat of the eruption is daily, but the actual item never comes, and so one develops a certain ambivalence about it. It was always like waiting for the last dull minutes of a boring sermon to end. There was no sin left in it, and none in ignoring it. You endured it only, but did not suffer, really.

Father had that Irishman that worked for him. The only one. He was as full of life as Father was full of worms. Father mocked him when he was not here.

There was a touch of the obsequious about the guy that my Father loved, or loved to hate, anyway.

"Oh, that Hibernian tugs his forelock and backs out of here like a serf, but you know he's in the tavern right now in his cups and laughing at me, and all his cronies with him. He'll never amount to anything."

Now the old man was done. Mother was gone two decades ago. It fell to me. I'll have nothing to do with this place. It had the smell of the grave in it when the paint was still tacky. The lawyers pushed the papers under my nose with the same dull mechanical mannerisms and basilisk expressions on their faces as their customer once showed to the world, but now he's laid out like a Pharaoh in the funeral parlor. I suppose they'll laugh later, chuckling over the fact they offered me a third of the value of the place, and I took it without hesitation.

I would have paid them to take it. I'm going to the tavern, to look for a man.

A Fresh Crop Of Rocks

DO YOU MISS the farm, Mr. Perkins?

"Are you daft? Why would I miss another year and a fresh crop of rocks?"

"Crop of rocks?"

"Have you never been where the trolley don't go? Do you think we pile those rocks along the plotlines to be picturesque for tourists?"

"I take your meaning, but it would seem that a fresh crop is out of the question."

"They grow right out of the ground every spring."

"Now you're having me on."

"You get frostbite standing in front of the icebox with the door open, don't you? Have you ever been on a farm?"

"A pig farm."

"They're all pig farms. Except on most, the farmer is the pig."

"I still don't get the fresh rocks."

"Nature provides, I tell you. But it never provides what you want when you want it. Above all, it provides rocks."

"How do they taste?"

"Like sweat. Every thing on a farm tastes like sweat."

"What about the rocks?"

"Look, the ground freezes hard here. Rock hard."

"I'm praying for a stony silence, now, myself."

"Well, you asked. The glaciers came through here a long time ago. Back before locusts and Republicans. And they spread rocks around. Mica schist, some; but granite boulders, mostly, made round by fighting amongst themselves.

Smooth as cannonballs, and hard enough to turn a plowshare into, well, not a sword, but not a plowshare anymore, either. It turns it into the raw materials a plow used to be made from."

"Look, Mr. Perkins, I get that part. But once they're stacked on the corners, and the plow salesman is retired on your money, that's about it, isn't it?"

"You'd think so. You'd think wrong. A farmer never thinks wrong. That's because a farmer never thinks his troubles are over. A farmer knows when he's eating a turkey with one hand and holding hands with a pretty girl with the other, things are going to go downhill soon. He feels about the same way when his hands are empty and the girl is ugly."

"My hands were always empty, and the girls were always ugly."

"That's the difference, see? At least the farmer's wife starts out pretty. The farm fixes that too."

"What about the rocks?"

"I told you, the ground freezes harder than a banker's heart every winter. Everything expands when it freezes. Except the rocks. They're held there, in the ground, and a little space opens up around them in the spring when the soil defrosts and shrinks. During mud season..."

"Mud season?"

"It's right after black fly time."

"Oh."

"Anyway, that sun gets to working, and the water trickles down into the earth with the heat, and fills in that tiny gap under that rock with the slurry and gurry. Almost imperceptible. Like getting a raise in the army.

After many a year, that rock starts to show up above ground, like a gopher with a bald head, and you've got to pry it out of there before you lose another harrow."

"I get you. A fresh crop of rocks. Why are the walls so low, then? Should be Egyptian-sized, by now."

"By the time your walls reach waist level using those devil's marbles, your great-grandson has moved to Nebraska to farm in peace."

"Speaking of slurry and gurry, let's go get some coffee at my house. There's no farming there."

Tommy Walnuts

I DON'T KNOW how many times I trudged up that hill with his lunch. Mother said he was kind to us when we needed it, so we need to look after him now that's he's alone. Me, I just do what I'm told.

I didn't know what to call him. He looked even older than he was, and he was nothing and nobody to me. He sensed it before I could figure out how to ask. He seemed to know everything about everything, although he never went out.

"Everyone calls me Tommy Walnuts."

OK, then. I'd sit in the milky sunshine next to the cobwebby window and watch him eat, while the cats -- his cats? -- the cats did figure eights through his legs. In all the time I was ever there I never saw him show the slightest interest in those creatures, but they hung by him like he was their mother. It was like he was the sun they orbited.

He never spoke while he ate. He'd murmur or grunt if you asked him a question, but shoot you a sort of withering look that made you refrain from asking another. When he was done, he'd take out a tin of tobacco and make himself a cigarette, and he'd smoke and he'd turn his eye towards yours, and it was like a signal that you could ask him something. He never asked me anything, except: How is your mother?

I can't explain what that man knew, because he seemed to know everything. I'd go to school and the nuns would try to pound the numbers and the words and some sense into my head. It took a lot of hammering; at least at first. But then I had a mission.

I wanted to ask this man something he did not know. I'd read at recess and at home and I'd sit in the library like a girl and scan the pages looking for the thing Tommy Walnuts would not know. I couldn't find it.

How long is the Great Wall of China? How do you calculate the hypotenuse of a right triangle? Who was the third vice-president of the United States? Did you know the Titanic had a sister ship?

"Two," he said, and send me home to scour the shelves again.

One day he looked rough. He always looked old and beat, but he seemed sick. He coughed a lot when he smoked.

"Are you all right?"

"I am always the same. Makes no difference. Ask your questions."

"How did you end up all alone here?"

He took a long drag on the cigarette. He looked around the empty room like a man on a stage surveying the audience before delivering his line. It was the first time he had ever even paused before answering me. I heard the clock tick, and the soft indistinct sound of a cat purring under his chair. A car sizzled past on the wet pavement outside.

He looked at me differently than before. I was sorry I had asked that. I'd gone too far. I was losing so I upset the board.

"I'm not alone. You are here."

Tommy Walnuts knew everything.

The Odd I Torium

STEP CLOSER FRIENDS. She won't bite you and I won't bite her. That's my wife. Don't be afraid to stare; I'm like one of Hoover's banks -- I've lost all interest. Poor woman caught her dress in a spinning jenny all those years ago in the factory, and was pulled straight through the loom. She come out the other end, unhurt, in a sort of miracle. But she's never spoken since, and moves like an automaton. We have the perfect marriage: a mute woman and a man that needs glasses. Don't be shy, push right on in.

Oh, we've got it, ladies and gents. We've got freaks and blockheads and five-legged goats. We've got Queen Zoe Zingari the Circassian princess, kidnapped from a harem and held here against her will by the Mauler of Mecca and Medina with his scimitar. She's got hair like a Brillo pad, and eyes that will bore a hole right through you. Step forward and see for yourself. You there, son, you look like you want to see a genuine Circassian tattoo. Will she show it to you? Give me a nickel and she'll show you. Give me a dime and she'll show me, too!

Like pigs to the slop now, wade on in, don't miss it. We've got the girl with the X-ray eyes, but when you see that raven-haired beauty you're gonna wish it was you that had the X-ray eyes -- but don't worry, boys, there's not that much standing between you and her. She can see through you like a bank inspector. Come on in!

We got the human pretzel over there and he's gonna show you more contortions than a politician from New Orleans on Judgment Day. Come on now, don't be shy. Move it on over.

Man, oh man, young lady we have the Prince of Fire and he's come all the way from Constantinople to set himself ablaze for you. He eats brimstone for his breakfast and leaves the privy vulcanized. Inside, outside, the fire makes no nevermind to this boy. Step on in and he'll show you who's hot. Go on, now, go!

Oh, I know what you're thinkin' He don't have a beautiful woman and a snake, does he? A boa snake from the Orinoco? Who don't? Not me! I do! Go and see it before it squeezes that little woman tighter than you would if you got the chance. You know, I might get a little tight myself later. It's hot in the sun. Get inside for your complexions ladies. Go!

Will you come with me to Africa? Will you come with me to Africa! Oh, they live closer to nature there than anywhere on God's green, don't you think so? They've made themselves into giraffes and they have their dinner plate with them always, but they forgot to go to the dressmaker's, if you take my meaning, sir.

We've got monstrosities. Curiosities. Hell, we've got atrocities. Push on in, ladies and gents, and leave me alone out here to wish I knew what was going on in there. Move it on over.

The Beer Is Gettin' Warm

FOUND MYSELF ON THE FLOOR all of a sudden. That was bad.

Potentially bad, anyway. It has a tendency to give a stiff bracer of courage to a fellow who's not quite sure of himself to see his man on the floor. If he gets hinky about you gettin' up, he might bring in the boot. And if he has hinky friends, well, they're all shod, ain't they?

All the dirt and corruption of the world is on the barroom floor, my mother would say. Now, I was no stranger to dirt and corruption, but I had no desire to get right down in it.

Still, a man could pause a short moment and take stock. I bet that fella is as surprised as I was to discover me down here. He's like a guy that prays in church but don't really believe it. He looks around halfway through, to see if anyone's gonna catch him at it. That's what he's doing now. You can never go halfway in church, sonny. And this is my church.

He thinks I'm old. He thinks it might be over before it started. He thinks I might not want any more of what's he's giving.

Son, I'm not going to get any more of what you've got.

He paused, and I did too. I hit my head on the way down somehow. There's nothing soft in a bar that ain't a woman, and in here, they're all pretty hard, too. They're lookin' on like any Roman would, watching the lions do their business.

Well I ain't a Christian right now, exactly. I kinda like the tingly feeling where I hit my noggin. It's not pain right now. Plenty of time for that tomorrow.

It's like a vibration; it's the soothing warmth of a rock that's had the sun beatin' on it all day. I feel it travel through me like a telegraph signal, to the very heart of my bones. And I feel Cuchulain in those bones.

Ah, well. I can't linger in the moment. Shame. A man's switch is on the outside, and only another can throw it. Roll over easy, like you might not get up, to get the right buffer. Then stand up, and put your fist one inch behind that feller's head. The beer is gettin' warm.

Rich Men Have Real Estate

MOMMA WAS QUIET. Daddy was silent.

I'd come home from school, and momma would hug me like she did. I could feel her snuffle on the top of my head. It was like she needed the smell of me, too. I'd sit in the chair in the kitchen, and talk and talk about the day, and she'd murmur along with me. It wasn't words, really -- just a little string of sounds to let me know she still heard her little yo-yo spinning, until I reached the end of my string.

I can't picture her face anymore in my mind's eye; I have to fish through the box of pictures to find one of her. I touch it when I look at it. I don't know why I run my hand over it but I do. I hear her murmuring all the days of my life.

Dad never spoke, or so it seemed. You could have hung a sign around his neck that read: I DON'T KNOW and saved the world a world of trouble. He said that all the time, when he said anything. I think it's funny that he almost always knew, but said that anyway. Daddy knew everything. Momma said knowing is in daddy's head, but it's in my mouth. He was alone all day in that field, and he got used to it. Or it got used to him.

I'd watch him wash the day's dust from his hands and face and the back of his neck while momma placed the dishes just so on the table. He seemed to linger over the basin a minute in an odd way. Daddy always seemed to move slow, but I noticed no one could ever keep up with him when he worked. I never could. I never will. I asked him why he liked to wash his face like that. He said, "Oh, I don't know." When daddy put an "oh" along with his *I don't know* it meant something different.

It meant he needed time to think, I think. Or maybe that meant he really didn't know. I don't know.

We sat in silence for a long minute at the table. I remember how the sun would slant in that window, the same angle every day plus a little or minus a little bit, and you could tell the time and the season by it. The afternoon would settle the air but the curtain would always sway like a dancer with it.

We worked at the food. Dad seemed all wrist at the table. His clothes never made it as far as he did. The teacher had told us about the lever you could use to lift the whole earth, and they all laughed at me when I said I'd seen it coming out of my daddy's sleeve. They all have fathers that don't say "I don't know" and their wrist fits in their sleeve and only lifts the newspaper.

Five minutes had gone by, easy, by the clock, and I could tell daddy was still turning over my foolishness in his mind. Why does a man wash any certain way? A man washes as much as momma makes him, and no more.

The oven cooled and ticked, the clock tocked, the glasses tinked, and a little breeze riffled through the curtains like a magazine. Daddy said, "A rich man like me has a lot of real estate, and carries it around with him. I like to take it off and look at it from time to time."

The Woodpile At Night

YOU'RE OUT THERE on the edge of it, and you know it.

You can smell it of course. The winter's waned to just a firm hand on the shoulder, not a fist in the face, and the dull swampy flavor of the place is revived a bit and washes over you when the wind shifts. Rotten and fecund. When it's frozen over, the wind tastes like metal, or an ice cube that's been in the freezer too long.

It rustles from time to time. A bird in a branch. A squirrel in the leaves. A possum or a raccoon or a bear or a griffon or a tyrannosaur, for all you know. They never announce themselves.

The good wood clanks when you drop it on the splitting stump. It sounds ceramic. You know it'll split along the medullary rays in one quick stroke, maybe a few stringy tendrils left to cleave the junks of wood together until they tumble to the hard packed dirt to wait for the stack. They arrange themselves neatly for a pile of bits born of something as eccentric as a tree; the gentle arc of the bark side always faces up to shed the water that sneaks under the pile cover, and produces the look of a grandstand of frowns.

The raptor often cruises overhead here. In the winter the sun is too low in the southern sky to put you noticeably in their shadow. The first you know of them is the shriek they emit, cruising way over the tall pines. No fish today. Something soft and furry that the cat missed.

Come out here at night, with the chilly stars pricked in the slate firmament, the wind abated. Come out to the edge of the forest and fen to the woodpile.

That edge has moved with the sunset, and you realize the new edge of the wild was the doorknob. You're in it now, not at the margin of it.

You can stand there a quiet minute, and all the sound seems gone but the roar of blood in your veins. The air is redolent of woodsmoke already, but something else, too. You're just another beast, without claw or tooth to speak of, and you're among them. You're not afraid; you're attuned to the prosaic place your kind once held in the order of things. You turn back to the path you crushed in the frosted dormant turf, and know the stuff of the cave.

A Thousand And One

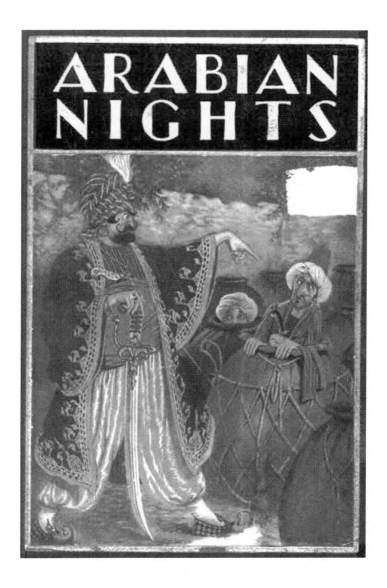

GRANPA TOLD ME all about the genie in the lamp.

It's the oldest story ever and came from the land of sand and the women with only eyes for you. It's in there, the genie of everything, but you have to find him and figure out how to let him out. He seems fussy but if you keep it simple and use your head he pops up like a daisy. Then he's out and you have to figure out what to do with him. Granpa says he's some kind of wonderful but as dumb as a stump, just like all of us. He can do anything but doesn't know what to do on his own. He needs guiding.

The lamp is always hidden in plain sight he says. Men go prospecting all over the landscape for the easy riches but they're generally lying right there on the ground for you to step over in your hurry and scurry to look for them. Granpa points to the men through the door of the grog shop and they're playing cards and Granpa says what good would it do for them to find the riches anyway.

In the library Granpa takes the books down from the high shelves that kids aren't meant to get at because the words in them are too dear to waste on such as us. He told me to run my hands over the cloth on the cover to see if it was the real deal inside. They don't waste the real nubbly cloth on the fakers.

The lady at the desk didn't like it but Granpa shushed her and we went home and opened that genie book but only so far. A book is like a man, Granpa says. You have to hold them both in respect. You can only bend a book or a man so far until they can't take it no more and then their back breaks.

Granpa says there's lots of men been bent back too far nowadays. They got told the only thing they could do didn't need doing anymore, and it broke them open and their hearts fell right out. They try to fill the hole with all sorts of things but nothing suits.

People act like thieves in reverse and put the broken books back on the shelf like nothing happened, but you can always tell because neither a man or a book can ever stand up straight any more after that.

Granpa said a body only needs a crust of bread today, it's true, but without at least the hope of a loaf tomorrow you're a goner. Scheherezade told that Sultan all those stories night after night and it kept her alive and me too.

It's Still Warm By The Stove

THEY COME, one after another. I wish they'd leave me be. It's still warm by the stove.

I've got tinder and wood 'til I'm gone and forgotten. The food always comes from the ground if you meddle in the dirt. Still they come and cluck their tongues and try to take me from my "squalor."

Squalor. I always loved that word. The pastor would boom it from the pulpit, and the newspaper would trot it out from time to time, back when they could still write, talking about some poor old soul and her countless cats. People don't understand thirty cats and one dish any more because they aren't on a farm with a pile of something worth eating in August they'd like to find still there in February.

I live in squalor so what. They come dressed like streetwalkers or *wandervogel* or something and want to save me from it. Save me from myself. How can anybody do that, anyway? It's not possible.

They don't know about the shades that tread the house with me. Gone to their reward. I could not go away from them until they invite me to join them. And I will not let you scrub their residue from my rooms.

I pray over their stones, including the blank granite stubs at your feet where we dared not write the names for fear of breaking our hearts over and over. But they have names in my heart, oh yes, they always did. I've whispered them in my own ear every day.

They come in their fancy cars, skinny with mindless exertions and not work, and want to expiate their guilt on the altar of my doorstep.

But you see, I know perfectly well that my life is like a coat that's gone shabby and threadbare, and I don't care. Many garments are not for show on a farm.

So my life is lived in squalor, and this must not be, you demand. But I take one look at you and know that maybe you never spent one moment in squalor, but your life is squalid. You're a gilt-edge leather-bound thirty-dollar Bible but all the pages are written by Beelzebub. Not the same, is it?

People didn't use to try to save you. They'd extend their hand and call you friend. I can't find that even in church anymore. Leave me be, by my little fire, to be warmed by the glow of the life I've lived. I'll not join you on your icebergs.

In My Cups

IN HIS CUPS, they said.

You're damn straight I am. I go there to keep from killin' those that smirk and murmur *in his cups* on the way to drink champagne and wine. Maybe the sinews stand out now as the flesh falls away with the passing of time but I could take them apart still.

These hands were given to me for something. Like curbstones they are, and ready always for work. But there is no work and hands like these can't pick up anything else now.

They scratched in their copybooks easy like, while I blotted mine, and that's the way life is. You're born to things. It's a Mohammedan way of life all around the globe. And so they lord over us by way of imperceptible shifts in the runes in a ledger, wear wool summer and winter, and look out the window at life like it's a picture with a name in the corner.

But they never stood for a moment with the big redwood bole poised between up and down, felt the pinch on the two-man, then heard the wonder of the gunshots of fibers letting go inside. The ground shakes when it comes down and you know you're alive -- if you can keep it. What do they know of the eastern sky in the desert when the sun retires? They never saw a fish, one hundred feet down in Tahoe, clear as day, nibble your hook.

They can make the greenbacks pile themselves to the transom without effort, but any printing press can do that.

There's supposed to be life in that money, other men's lives stored like the fire that hibernates in a log until you strike the match. They couldn't get it out without men like me.

The creatures -- the live creatures, not those cadavers – the children and the kittens and the women all come to me, because I got the life in me, always, banked low now but still there. I'll tell you all about it. When I'm in my cups.

Infinite Calculus

THERE WAS A PROCESS for everything.

I remember long, languid, early summer afternoons in mathematics class. The teacher would drone while the cicadas chirruped outside the window. The equation was chalked on the board and the intricate steps of logic would be parsed from it. I'd stare at nothing out the window and remember her. Her equations were no less perfect.

The chair was placed just so. The toy was brought. The neighbors waved, and got their wave in return. The sun was in the right place to warm the side yard. When a button lost its moorings, there was a moment of recognition, and as inexorably as anything Newton could come up with, the tray was produced; the color of the thread adduced and deduced; the problem solved. She'd always hum while she did anything -- not musical, exactly, more like a machine that is running just right. It was mesmerizing.

Her hand was delicate, but strong and practiced. Her whole life was like a roller at the summer beach. Quietly moving forward. There was power in it, but not made evident by anything showy. It was the residue of a million unseen forces distilled to an inevitability. You sensed very young that it would be very difficult to swim against its force, and pointless; so you turned your face to the sun and rode it instead.

I never understood why she introduced a variable like me into her life's equation, but after a while I realized that a mind like hers could not be satisfied with simple arithmetic.

The Rusty Bucket

I LIKE THE WATER from the rusty bucket best. It tastes like something.

It tastes like the earth. I can feel it. I roll it around in my mouth and it's like the magnetism of the poles is in it. The world and everything in it is in the well.

I love that baby. I want to bathe him in the water from the rusty bucket. I want to baptize him myself from the font of the world. I want his bones to sing with the vibrations in the earth. Not clean, exactly. Anointed.

The boy's father carries him like a package. He isn't anything to him yet. He loves him, sure, but in a potential sort of way. At least he carries him like there's something breakable in that package. His love is purer than mine, because it is all in his mind, and still he loves that baby. Me, I can still smell the musk of my own womb on his soft little head. And a taste of the rusty bucket.

I didn't know what to think when they strung the power lines across the horizon. Whatever is in those wires is not a person, but it trespasses just the same. But then I felt it. There was power in them, coursing through them. It was everybody and everything going everywhere all the time.

Sometimes I take my boy out in the cool of the evening, the clank of the final fork on the last plate still ringing in the house behind us, and we drink from the bucket with the rust in it, and I hold him up in the air so he can be washed in the power of those lines.

I was born to drink from that bucket. He was born to live in that power.

Big Mistake

WELL AFTER ALL his help was gone, or gone to mold, he'd still descend the stairs like some kind of baron. You'd have to wait there like a peon, hat in hand. Hat in hand wasn't just an expression to him. If he came down and you had a hat on your head in his lobby, he'd turn right around without speaking. Back when he had a flunkey or maid or the like with a palm you could grease to smooth it over for you, you had a chance to get another crack at him. On your own? Forget it.

He held the sway of money over everybody. You'd open your folio only after stumbling through the mummery of manners that his great impassive face seemed to demand, and steering the boat of commerce through any shoals of etiquette required for the occasion was entirely up to you. He'd never utter a sound. I resented it at first – silently, alone in a room with the shades drawn, maybe -- but after a while I realized that even listening to your entreaties was his only way of acknowledging you as a fellow human. If he had no business with you, you simply didn't exist.

He wasn't short, but he'd always stand on the last step coming down. You'd have to hold out the papers on the folder or your briefcase lain on its side on your palms, and he'd take out his pen and sign. Or not. He'd never ask a question or answer any. It was expected that it would all be on the paper. God help you if it wasn't.

He signed every paper with the solemnity of a ceremony for the founding of some great state. His handwriting was perfect, if a bit florid. It was his art.

The city went to hell and gone all around him. He'd never go outside, and after his retinue lit out or died on his vine, the place took on a ramshackle and gloomy aspect. The local kids ransacked the neighborhood like the barbarians they were, and even sawed the little five-pointed nuts from the tops of the fire hydrants for the nickel they could get for the brass. They might die in an unquenchable fire a week later in their tenement hellholes, but a nickel's a nickel. It was a metaphor and meaningless at the same time. They'd generally break anything they couldn't steal, out of boredom as much as any kind of malice, I suppose, but not one of them dared to even approach that house, even after the old man died.

It was left to me to close up his affairs. I was astonished to find that he never really had any money, at least that I could find. He possessed the ability to size up the world in some unseen way and simply send a note to our modern-day counting house, offering to broker some arcane shift of numbers from one column to another in some hidden ledger, and the people I worked for knew his name on the paper would make it happen. His name and acumen alone was the key in all those locks. I had to go back to the old place and look around for anything that might point to a trove somewhere, but the place was as barren as a grave. I could feel the dead weight of his soul in that house. I sat in church every Sunday, and even with the thurible swinging right under my nose, the chorus rising up from the back of the nave like a thunderhead, the Latin chants rolling across the pews like scudding clouds and the wafer disintegrating in my mouth, I felt nothing.

Stand inside that guy's door for half a minute and you felt like you just broke the seal on a mummy's tomb -- one that maybe you should have passed on by. He was a dread god, my signatory.

My boss told me the man with the fine fist and the granite face was once filled with bonhomie. He'd travel and sip champagne with dinner and smoke big cigars after his deals were struck. He was in Delmonico's in New York, and the waiter handed him a card. His only daughter had died of the influenza. He never said a word, just dropped the card on the table and went back to his house and never left it again that anyone saw -- until they carried him out. If you ask me, he never left it.

The maid from back in the forties that drank a bit and got flirty told me *sotto voce* that he wouldn't even let a curtain be drawn back from the windows, because he said he'd seen a face -- the face of his little girl, the girl he left behind with some duenna and the fever -- in the garden.

They'll knock it down, probably, because no one will buy it. He isn't around to put his name on the deal, after all, and his name was all there ever was to it, I guess.

I locked the door and made my way to the street with brambles tugging at my cuffs the whole way. I teetered a moment on the edge of the curb, the demarcation between the spidered asphalt and the sidewalk spangled with gum, and took a long bracing drag of stale city air to clear my head before pushing off to the train. I knew I shouldn't, but everybody touches the stove once or twice in their life. I looked back at the house. Big mistake.

What Time It Ain't

WHAT THE HELL time is it?

Doesn't really matter, I expect. The rhythm of the day, the coming and receding of it tells you all you need to know. The whistle will blow when the time matters again. Then you'll know what time it is. What good does it do to know what time it ain't?

I love it here in the morning. You walk down the decline through the pines, the soft, gentle shush-shush of the big needles grinding under your boot, the fog swirling around your feet and dashing off a bit and then collecting itself again in your wake, waiting for the sun to rise and put it to bed. It reminds me of Pa blowing smoke rings on a long winter's evening. The stars are out strong though the sun is near to come. The idiot woodpeckers haven't begun, but you hear the songbirds a bit, sensing the sun waiting on the platform for the day to begin. They know what time it is.

I used to have a watch, but the steam, the sap, the turps, the cosmoline --well, they did those little marvels in, one after another. After a while, you just let things go. I don't need a watch to stand over the machine and feed it like some dragon puffing steam, the great jeweled drops of amber sap boiling out like a bit of food on its smacking lips.

No one wanted to feed the beast. It roared and clanked and hissed and bit off the odd man's fingers. You had to be first every day in the dawn to fire her up and bring the gauges up like Vulcan's clocks. Once it was going you could never stop. It would pull itself to pieces with its unremitting greedy chewing if there was nothing in its maw.

Oh, I'll take her. It's my one, true love. A man can love a thing he understands, it's true, and seeks the whole world over for the thing that understands him in return. The steam in the beast's veins courses through its body like life does in any man's husk, and it understands me.

I feed it and it feeds me. I'll lie on my bed someday all broke down from my exertions and feel the Lord's hand on my shoulder and wish I had one more day of the smell of the loblolly pine in my nose. Give me Extreme Unction with turpentine, Father.

E Tan E Epi Tan

OH GAWD SAVE ME or I'm beaten.

I sees the shadow of the whole crowd in the bowl hanging over me. I hears the animal roar, the lust to see another man's stuffin'. They'd have cheered me like me own mother if I stood over the rubbish of his corpse and the referee raised me fist instead. Now it's jeers.

All fours. He hit me again when I was on all fours. He already hit me low. Bit me. Spit at me. It signified nothing. I'd have killed him for the money. I'd have climbed from the ring and killed his family for a finnif. I'll kill him still in the alley like a git-em-up guy for the money if I get the chance.

All fours and the blows stop. There's a ringing but I'm OK anyway. There's a light in my eye that I know ain't really shining, and I'm part blind with it. I can feel him standing over me. His sweat is dripping on me. If I put one foot flat on the canvas he'll hit me like a train; if I roll over the referee will end it.

The crowd is like lions when the zebra stumbles. They're on me too. I never been beaten before. I don't know what to do. How to act. They teach you how to be a loser at school but here you only get to learn it the hard way.

There can be a long time in every tick of a clock. I remember the nuns years ago and the drowsy hot afternoons. My head is like that again, with the buzzing. They tried, oh they tried to get the numbers and dates and spelling into my head, but I was born a gone gosling. The words always swum in front of my mind's eye in a jumble like a carousel at night. They said that boy's gonna grow up with no ideas but bad ones, but there's nothing for it. He's a dynamiter at heart.

One thing I remember from them dusty old books: *Come back with your shield, or on it.* I liked that. A mother of Sparta was Irish, I guess, and who knew?

If they carried me out of here dead after the head and head game was settled I'd rest peaceful for a thousand years. No worries. But there's no mercy in being beaten like this. I'll live, and the little faces will arrange themselves around the table tomorrow. The wife, the loogan's wife, she'll look at me hangdog and the bowls empty, and say nothing. If she said something we could shout and break the furniture over winding up back of the fifteen ball again. But she knows better than that, and she'll turn mute. I'll whisper I'm a dirty nose over and over to myself but she'll never say it. She don't have to.

I look up into the glare. There's a halo around his head like a stain glass window when you go to confession. The referee is bringing his arm down like a poleax, over and over, with the counting. How many? I don't hear. He takes his time and only calls the fouls after the blood is drawn, but now he's all business and he counts like a prison clock, 'cause he's a hundred-percent heel.

I look up at the johnny-come-lately's face in the halo. He's afraid I'll get up. I'm afraid to stay down.

How can I lose?

Three-Quarter Cape

I **REMEMBER HER** laughter drifting out through the kitchen window. It was always muffled even before the trip through the house distilled it. Grandma would never let it all out. She laughed a lot, and smiled most of the rest of the time, but never with abandon. She'd glow with it like a lamp in a house at night.

Grandpa never spoke. I never met a man more like the Sphinx. He had a grin that wasn't there. Halfway between smiling and just plain looking at you. He could have been a fool, I guess; his silence could have covered up for a million inane things he might have said, after all. But somehow I doubt it.

The grass was always hay by the time I showed up. Each blade a tree in a miniature forest. I'd get out the rusty push mower and meditate over the swish swish swish of the blades. The daylilies would sway like hula dancers in the sea breeze and I'd dance the rigid right-angle minuet of the landscaper beside them. After you cut the grass it looked like a balding man's crew cut. It's all sand anyway.

Grandma would bring you out a glass of lemonade. I remember it precisely, though it was long ago. Her eyes were weary and her hand trembled, so one time it would be a sort of liquid lemon praline, and the next a jolt of lemon battery acid. But it was ice and lemons mashed by her hand and gobs of sugar from the same chipped bowl your mother dipped her spoon in to dust her cereal back when U-Boats cruised off the coast there. It was a taste of forever, unchanging. I'll never forget it.

All gone now, of course, but for the totem of the house. The time has long since passed that's needed to take the sting of it being empty from everyone. We all own it, so no one does, and we each go and shear the lawn once in a while, and chase out a raccoon or a squirrel that managed to find a way in. We swim in the tepid ocean and drink at the little shack on the access road with the blue-hairs and the fishermen. Maybe an afternoon on the butt-sprung couch or a night sleeping on one of the musty mattresses in the cobwebby bedrooms. Then back to the world over the bridges.

"A Three-Quarter Cape," my Grandmother would gently correct you, if you called her house a Cape.

Maybe I should open the house again. I feel three-quarters Cape again, too.

The Young Man Don't Know Nothing

YOU SEE, the young man comes in here and he don't know nothing. That's a given.

Well, not precisely nothing. He knows all sorts of things. It's just that everything he knows isn't so, or isn't worth a fart in a whirlwind to have rattling around in your head. Useless.

A young man isn't born to be useless. You've got to make him so. A young man is born into this world to be a boon to his fellow man and a credit to his parents -- if his parents don't pay too much attention to him and ruin him. Let him be.

They come all in here, one after another, extravagant of hair and miserly with manners. They want to start right in being something. They want to nuzzle up at the front of the pig right off. Son, you're an unthrowed pot. Stand up straight and listen.

You see, you're not born knowing, and you can't learn much useful from a book. How you gonna know to put fabric softener in the steam box to make the oak come out of there real withy and limber? Your grammar school teacher don't tell you that out here in the real world you gotta use the ceiling for a brace for the inner stem while you make down the bolt.

Oh, a smart one or two do come in, though not as often as you'd like. Often enough, maybe, to remind you how dumb you were when you were their age. They're young and handsome and clever and the whole world stretches out to their horizon. You're already on the horizon and you know it.

You think to yourself how wise beyond his years that boy is to come in here and stand up straight.

He's wearing the wrong clothes and toting a comical box of the wrong tools, and not enough of them, either, and his hands are like his momma's, or more likely his daddy's if he's an ink-stained wretch. He's wrong, all wrong, and in every aspect and from every vantage point-- asleep or awake; in action or repose; drunk or sober -- but he's smart enough to look you straight in the eye and say, "I don't know nothing but I'm willing to learn if you'll show me."

A boy like that knows everything.

She Called It The Piazza

SHE CALLED IT the piazza. I'd been to the library and it isn't a piazza at all, but she says it just the same.

I didn't say that, but it's not like I know what to call it anyway. I wouldn't say it to her face if I did know because she is so fierce. The doctors, like bad farmers, pulled babies and other things you'd think were vital out of her and all sorts of bits off of her as the calendars repeated themselves, and father says when they bury her there will be an echo inside. She carries on like the turning of the earth, and everyone loves her and fears her no matter how much of her is left.

She never went leathery; she got adamantine. She was a basilisk to a stranger and a pitted madonna to her own. We make a pilgrimage, no less, to visit her. *Which one are you again* is the name she uses to prove she loves us all the same amount. She presses a quarter in my hand like a card trick when we leave.

The piazza is just a rotten porch that leans drunkenly off the building and she sends me to get the food that cooled out there. It's thirty rickety feet above the jetsam of a thousand lives gone bad, surrounded by chainlink and crime. She's like a one-woman congress, overruling all sorts of laws of man and nature, but you can't help feeling she can't keep a lookout for gravity forever on your behalf, can she? Everything is only a matter of time in this world.

It's always hot and close when you return, breathless from fear and hurry and the whip of the wind, and you notice she has only two colors: grey and the pink of her cheek. There are always things I don't understand, boiling. Everything on the plates is grey and pink, too.

The rooms are in a parade. The triptych of the parlor windows shows the sack of a forgotten Rome through the tattered lace. No running in the hall! Her daughter lives down stairs so there was no one to bother but… the very idea!

But how could any child linger in that tunnel of a hall? You had to get past it to the kitchen table. The bedrooms branched off, dim caves that smelled of perfume bought in stores forty years closed by men thirty years dead. The indistinct whorls on the wallpaper reached out to touch your hand like a leper.

At the table, the lyre-back chair groans and shifts under even my little weight, and you sit transfixed while she spoons the sugar and dumps the milk into the tea until the saucer is a puddle, and you wondered in your head how many times the bag could take it. There's cinnamon and laughter now and then and blessed sunlight that turned the battered battleship linoleum into a limpid pool. The cork shines through the scrim of the coating, a million footfalls revealing more and more of it over time.

And Catherine? The Cork shows through there, too.

Fog In New Beige

WHY DO YOUR FOOTSTEPS sound that way in the fog?

In the broad daylight, they get swallowed up like Jonah. They mix in with the clatter of the cars and Clark's old wagon and the kid with the roller skates and the ding-ding of the faraway trolley. At night in the fog, they ricochet around and I hear them like gunshots. They are mine -- and another's, too.

He's followed me around in the fog these three years. I can't scrape him off in the Bethel or the tavern or even the little place with the greasy balls of opium from Marracech that erases everything else from your mind. I'd beat my head on these granite flags if I thought it would do any good. I know he's there, but he's drowned out all day, every day. It's the night and the fog that puts him on your shoulder, and we dance together down the street like ball-room winders.

A man will go over the side from time to time, and no mistakin'. I've been fished out twice myself. You stand there shivering every which way as your mates have a jolly moment, then you work the rest of the day soaked to your tallow as a reminder of where you might be sleeping. But there is no sleep there, if the fog is any measure.

The man's hand was in mine. Rough as his language. His whole wrist. I could feel the blood pumping through his veins. I felt the tug of the wake trying to yank him under the foam by his boots. But I had him, sure. His big, stupid, moonpie face, with thirty winters written on it, looked up at me, glowing white in the fog.

And then I sneezed, and when that strange, unwonted spasm passed, I found I had two hands on the rail, and he was gone.

A man that goes over at night has no right to hope to be saved. *One hand for me, and one for the boat* doesn't cover it at night on the shoals. It's two hands for the boat at night. I threw everything on deck over the side and yelled to raise the dead and we had that boat turned hard about in a minute flat. We could have saved a half-dozen assorted Jonahs and Ahabs -- at noon. He was long gone in the fog at night.

We heard him calling for a good, long while, but in a fog, where does a noise come from? I can still hear him now, and see that look on his brother's face, measuring me there on the deck when the voice faded.

Like always, there are two footfalls for every one in the fog. I wander down the hill, the stone slabs of the sidewalk rising up and appearing under my feet like continents on a map. This road is busy in the early day, but we're all alone here in the fog. No need to keep a lookout for a car to come along and hit me; I could lie down here and wait all night. Why bother to look? You can just drift across the lanes.

I always loved the sound of the chestnut plank under my foot. You can feel the pier shift a little with the slop of the slack tide. It's like the world breathing in and out.

I walk to the end, and reach out for his hand one more time.

The Ten Fingers

AN OLDER BROTHER is a sacred thing, Father told me. Just so. But he doesn't know the half of it. Father's older brother went west on him and disappeared. Maybe he's in California. He doesn't know, but he says he cares.

I care about Noah. He's my older brother. Mother says he was born in the biggest thunderstorm ever, and Mother knew he'd be taciturn, because Noah didn't say a word all day.

Sometimes I think Mother is pulling on my leg.

Noah doesn't talk much around Father, but no one but me does anyway. Mother says the oldest is usually the wisest. Maybe so. I talk all the time, she says, even when I'm sleeping, but how is a body supposed to know that? I used to hide checkers in my cheeks and put them back on the board when Noah wasn't looking, and he must have known that, but like always, he just smiled and carried on, quiet-like. I think he must always talk to himself in his head, so the words don't build up and cause a jam.

Noah knows I'm little; I don't think Father knows. Father tells me to do things, then turns his back to me and goes back to what he was doing. It's usually Noah that turns my head around to the chore Father told me to look at in the first place, when I get distracted -- and not with the cuff Father thinks I need, either.

When I was awful sick, and Father was away to Lafayette, Noah carried me all the way to the doctor's brick house, because the fever made Mother worry so. Noah's always carrying me, it seems, because he knows I'm little.

Father works too hard. He takes the trees, one by one. There isn't but one gnarly tree left in the barnyard. All the branches hang too high for me to reach. I ask Father, but he never seems to listen; but I never even have to ask Noah. He never says a word. He just sees me there, and finds a way to pass by, no matter what he's doing, and weaves his fingers together like a sling and gives me the "ten fingers" to the branch that's lowest. He just does it, and walks on, wordless. I bet Father doesn't even know he does it. But I know.

I asked Mother why Father doesn't always hear me, but Noah hears me before I talk, I think. Doesn't Father care for me, Mother? She said, "Hush, Father made Noah for you, he loves you so much, to give you the ten fingers without asking."

How Father knew I'd need ten fingers, before I was even born, well, Mother didn't say. I don't dare ask Father anything. He's a good man, my Father, I guess; but why does he have to take all the climbing trees?

Noah came to me and said, "I have to go now," just like that.

"Where do you have to go? To Lafayette?"

"No. To the war, down South, to do my part."

"But you can't go. Who'll give me the ten fingers?"

"There's others, brother, that need my ten fingers now. I'll go and give it to them. Then I'll come home, I promise. Maybe you won't even need the ten fingers by then. I made you this, to give you ten fingers when I'm gone." Noah gave me little wooden steps he had fashioned, to reach the branch, and the bed, and the wash bucket.

Father cried when Noah left, already dressed in his blue uniform, to give the southern man ten fingers. I never saw Father cry before.

I think it's because he's got no brother to give him the ten fingers anymore.

Spring Potatoes

" **PA, HOW DO YOU** get the coverin' disks to hit the furrow?"

"They jest do, son."

"But you never look, pa."

"Keep your eyes on the horizon, boy. Sound advice always."

"But how do you know?"

"Waste of time to tend to that which tends itself, son. Got to trust to God and yourself. Who else you gonna trust, exactly?"

"How did you learn what goes on behind you?"

"Same as you, son -- riding along and asking a lot of damn fool questions. My own father said that if the nattering ever stopped behind him, he'd know enough to turn the rig back towards the house and arrange a funeral. He knew nothing else would shut my piehole."

"You've gone quiet now, pa."

"What a man says has meaning, son. You need to choose your words careful. Can't get two drinks in you on Saturday night and start a fight with a neighbor you might need a hand from someday. Makes a man pick through his words first, like picking through the taters looking for eyes. It doesn't pay to broadcast words or seeds if the potential for good isn't in them, or the ground is likely to be barren in the first place. Children can talk as they like."

"I'm a man now, pa."

"Shaving doesn't make a man, son. You'll go quiet in your turn. Don't rush it. Heh. Why don't you work up the courage to talk to that girl, the one from away, at the Grange Hall fetes a bit first.

If you dawdle, you'll never get someone to hound you from the back of the tractor for your own.

And sakes -- keep your prayer handles between the hoppers or you'll muck up the line. I can feel it."

Take Your Image

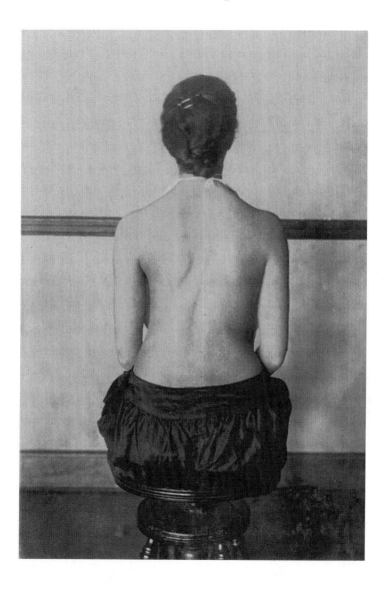

TAKE THE IMAGE, you blighter.

Am I not what you need? My gammy back's a corkscrew, and me a culchie to boot. A man could lift a girl out of it, couldn't he -- if he was a good skin. But you're Cromwell's men all over again, aren't you?

Oh, yes, me spine is banjaxed to beat the band. But still, you're not at nothing, are you? Trolling the locals and asking for the girls that are bent. You can wear your white coat and your pince-nez and jot on the paper but I've seen you looking, haven't I, now? Put your shift in the press, you said in a voice pitched like a lookout in an alley, and your eyes were on me proper straight away, weren't they?

I'm not like the ignorant savage who thinks you're stealing his immortal soul through your lens, no. I know better. But we Hibernians are all bent from the rickets, and so you can put naught but a dingy coin in my hand and for you it's *Bob's your Uncle* but for me it's nothing but shame and half a meal. Take the image.

I'm bent but my fanny is there and I could drop bairns like apples from a tree if our Lord and Saviour himself hadn't pissed on my chips and made me a freak, good for nothing but the attention of such as you. You! Dry as dust, and half as wholesome as a vampire.

Take your image.

The Fish No Coom

IT NO COOM.

All of life passes by on the way to somewheres else now, but it no coom.

The fish no coom anymore. They'd coom and leap into the seine, they would, without a care for themselves, and us without a care for them. All banished now.

We'd dig in the muck for the shells of St. James, and the excursionists would ooh and aah over the beastly things. We'd titter at our treasure and eat kale from the back acre and spend the money on trifles. All gone now. Even the Brahmins won't venture out here any more. The money don't coom.

She tells her mother and her friends I am a good man as I don' t strike her and I don't drink my wages. But there are no wages if the fish don't coom, and I'm not any particular sort of man at all if I don't drink only because I have nothing.

The ocean took my digit in the bight of the rope in a gale once. It was nothing, really. Just a pinch. After a while the pinches add up, though, don't they?

The clock ticks and I wait. I'm filled with shame that's like an anger at nothing and no one. The fish don't coom, but I know she will coom when her day is done, and accuse me with the turning of the knob.

The New Churchill

OH YEAH. JUST. "Accommodated." Beautifully put. The place is full of men never cracked a spine except in a fight, and the proprietor puts up a sign that reads: ACCOMMODATED. How about: PUT UP, and PUT UP WITH? Farmed? Stacked like cordwood? Buried like a Pharoah's handlers -- still alive, but not going anywhere?

I climb the steps feeling like those Aztec fellows must have felt on the way to the top of those big stone wedding cakes they were partial to, in line to have their hearts tugged out – we were both born to appease some god with a perpetual toothache. The world is more of a theoretical place now, but that just means you can have your heart extracted every day and it grows back for the next. Like Sisyphus in the schoolbook. No, that's the guy with the rolling stone. No matter; it's the same sort of story, anyhow.

There's no call for stacking one stone atop another right now, never mind just rolling one around. The last stone we got to push uphill got rolling a pretty good clip, and a body got winded real fast chasing it down the hill. After a while, perhaps a regular guy can be forgiven for thinking he might like to stop to rest for a spell, then try again later. By the time he's picked himself up and dusted himself off, that rock has rolled all the way out of sight. But even a man prone to fooling himself can't help but notice that the place he chose to stop and rest has a row of bottles behind the counter.

The house itself is like a woman grown old, missing a few teeth, gone thick and manly. But you can tell the ruin used to be something. The old frame shows something of the heretofores.

I heard tell a captain of local industry built it to prove to everybody that he had finally made it big in this old world. He said prove it to everybody, but really meant to himself, I'll bet. The bank took it from him the minute a dark cloud appeared on the horizon, and showed him that the world has no opinion. Now find somewhere else that'll accommodate you. The old dust-catcher and soul-collector is currently accommodating the men who heard about the fishing or the potatoes or the blueberry farms or the logging. Trouble is, they heard about two decades ago.

The inside shows nothing of the exalted past except the ghostly outlines on the plaster where every bit of the extravagant gimcrack was removed. If it was worth a damn, they pulled it out and reassembled it in a big, new house in Washington, D.C.; no doubt to prove to someone else that they've finally made it in this world by presiding over the desolation of a lost one. Fitting.

The bank stuck a hard guy behind a counter in the front hall that doesn't care if you pull a razor or a roscoe or a long face or whatever. He collects the money if you got it, or your scalp if you don't. I like him, though, because he treats me the same as the rest. We do our business and he pushes the key across the pockmarked counter and there's no accusation in it. No kindness. Nothing.

It's the nothing you crave. It's -- accommodating.

Das Is Culch

"WHAT? What did you say?"

I felt like someone a few minutes after a punch in the face. The sting's gone out of it, but you're dizzy or something. Everything's blurry around the periphery; you're looking through a kind of tunnel at one thing or another, but each standing in a line, a sequence. It doesn't knit itself into a whole for you. Was this fellow speaking German to me? I speak German. That doesn't mean anything.

Dad's dead, in some strange place among strange men. He wasn't even here when he died. The timber and the blueberries and every other damn thing they do to keep body and soul together around here played out and dad breathed his last on a rusty boat dragging what-all to god-knows-where. They sewed him in his canvas bag and slipped him in the ocean like a card trick.

I never understood that whole wake thing until now. Your loved one made up by some insane hairdresser and laid out like a buffet of sorrows in the parlor. People who hated the stiff, dropping by to make sure he's dead and to say what a lovely specimen he always was, the words turning to ashes in their mouths to save your ears the trouble. You just stand there bewildered. A month later you'd take your own life or join the circus or weep while watching *What's My Line*. You're just numb when it's fresh in your memory. Human nature comes with its own novocaine, but those teeth are coming out. Hard. It's an odd and disturbing tug at the point of attack; the ache comes later. But at least now I see why you want to see the husk a last time. I'm not sure if you pinch the corpse or yourself to gauge who's alive and who's not.

Well I was at the point where you can't help yourself; you probe the hole over and over with your tongue where the molar came out, each time only half-believing it's gone, wondering if you'd have taken better care of it maybe it'd still be there. It doesn't hurt, really; it's tender and offers a sort of mute reproach when you touch it. So here I am, up from Boston, the closest civilization, but not close at all, and I have questions no man alive can answer for me.

"I say dat's 'is culch."

I could hear the French in it now. Not like France French. I've met Algerians and Vietnamese and people from the Caribbean and when they speak French it sounds like Paris. This fellow is Canadian French. His accent sounds like a wild animal passing a poorly-digested hiker out in the woods. He is, like everything here in northern Maine, barbarous.

"He says that's his culch. Your father's culch."

The French fellow slunk back into the bowels of the rude sort-of dormitory we were in, and this other voice presented himself. He was tall and rangy and a little dirty; compared to the little bearded homunculus prone to the German-sounding French grunting, he looked and spoke like a Roman senator. He was as self-possessed as the other fellow was chary. No one introduces themselves here, I notice. They seem to know what everyone's about, without asking, and speak to you as necessary and no more. If they don't know you, you don't belong here, and it's but a moment's work for them to figure out what your story is. Who else would hover at a dead man's empty bed in a lumber camp?

"What language is that? What does that mean?"

There was that languid pose all these men have around here. There's a blank look you can't make out any emotion in. You start to imagine all sorts of thoughts it might signify, but because it's so blank, and lasts for so much longer than polite society would allow, it might mean anything. He might think you a fool or a king. Or maybe's he's not thinking about you at all. Dad was like that, what little I knew of him. Impenetrable.

"It's not any sort of language a man would know unless he needed to know it. It's his stuff. Stuff a man keeps 'cause he can't bear to part with it, but knowing in his heart it's worthless. He can't leave it out and about or it would be thrown away in the rubbish by anybody else. So he puts it in a little spot near the midden he sleeps in, and no one touches it, and pretends not to notice it, neither."

And there was a fly tied for a fish that would never see it; a compass without a needle; a few dog-eared books too tired for the library -- not much really, a few bits of broken this with a missing that. And a wedding ring with no finger in it, and a picture of me.

The Writer

WHY WOULD I tell you how I do it?

They always ask. I'm never more creative than when they ask. They dutifully write it down with their tongue showing in the corner of their mouth. They're not bright enough to look up into my face, even once, to see the twinkle in my eye. The jo-school drudges will read it, take it as gospel, and preach it, brother -- oh brother. Can't do any of them any harm, as nothing can do them any good.

I'd tell them the bald truth, I really would, if they'd have it. But it's all kabuki. Anything that smacked of coloring outside the lines would send them reeling. Animals lash out in all directions when they're spooked. Can't risk it.

They talk to me in hushed tones about the tomes, but it's not that. They want the money. They want every woman at a cocktail party standing in line behind movie stars, all waiting to talk to the great scribe. They want the trappings. They don't care a fart for the logos. They should get a job.

They'll coast pretty fair for a while. They'll fuss over the text born into their life's haversack, writing and rewriting: dad was mean and mom ran off with the plumber. They'll grow dissipated and wait for another set of mother and father and the plumber to show up. Maybe they can write about waiting for a little while.

Writer's block. Hilarious. It's work, you dolts. You sit down and you put the words on the paper. Or you don't. That's it. You never had an instinct for anything that didn't step right on your toe and announce itself. I'll not waste my time tracing the shapes in your palm.

Coal Breaker

THE GREAT MAN'S house. The daughters of the men who cracked his anthracite cracked oysters for him in there. The girls would come home and say they had a place in the great man's house and would rub shoulders with quality, pa. The fathers knew him, though. A werewolf. A vampire. They would sit silent with their black faces and their watery eyes at the kitchen table and know what it meant to turn your children over to such men. They'd say nothing because there was nothing to say.

They turned their sons over to the collieries. There was honor there -- and shame. A man hopes for better for his children than he got. Nothing ever gets better in a mine. You come out every day like the womb. Born again. Or not. The great man would read of the little men like insects that worked in his seams, dead of the gas or the great hand of gravity. It was a story from far away, as their very daughters cracked his oysters.

The men would see their sons fight back the plain fear that showed in their eyes as the sky passed away and the rank earth swallowed them for their labors, and feel pride, too. No man is ashamed of his son at his elbow in a mine. He is ashamed of himself, maybe.

What is a man to do? A Welshman might as well be a black ant. He's got the instinct to go down and up in that little hole and he can't help himself. He knows no other thing until he knows nothing forevermore. He does what he does. And the great man did what he did. He saw the man's weakness, and his strength, and used one to get the other.

The great man had the other great men in his pocket.

He could call out the guard on a whim. He could kill a man legal. He could kill him any which way. He could do as he pleased. He could live in the shadow of a boneyard in a palace and there were none dared to squeak. The men said we'll vote and stick together, and the great man just put one more man in charge of them, the new black prince of the county with the thing with the letters behind him. It was organized, but not like you'd think. Things would go on behind a velvet curtain. If they drew it back you'd see the smirk of the hyena in there.

Then there was no work. The union and the boss alike said no coal. The big machines and the kept men kept even the culm from us. The great man couldn't mine the coal by himself, so he mined the banks and the government and the union and got his gelt just the same.

The great man thought he knew men. But he did not know your father and his father. They knew the coal like he knew his oysters. They went into the woods where the seams lay close to the sky, and they began again. The very earth gave them what they always sought. The men sent to find them and stop them joined them instead. The trucks ran at night to the great glittering city where the coins slept in great vaults.

The housemaids knew from where it came, for they had come from there themselves. They pressed the coins into the dingy hands at the alley gate and burned it in their own great man's house. Their little hods filled with bootleg coal made a pyre for our great man.

The great man's house. Look on it.

One Quarter Rich

HE WOKE UP one morning and felt strangely. The sun slanted in through the curtains in the usual way. Birds chirped. That sort of thing. That wasn't it.

He lay there for a good long time and tried to sort it out. He hadn't made a decision. That would be silly. Claiming you decided any such thing would be like claiming you'd decided to have a heart, or a liver. No, it was recognition of a bare fact that he had rolling around in his head. Something overlooked. A toy you forgot you owned until you trod on it, barefoot, in the dark. You're not glad you found it, exactly, you're -- very aware of it. You know it intimately, immediately; after all, there's an impression of it in your flesh just then as you hop and mutter. He luxuriated under the covers for a while turning it over and over in his mind. It had no seam; no crack; no blemish. He was made perfect by it. It was inspiration. Thinking without volition.

He was fourteen. Powerless, fourteen is. A dog to be kicked. When the adults were through pretending to mold your character by using you as a coolie, any one of your contemporaries with five pounds more muscle than you would pick up the slack and push you around. You know what a woman is for, but unfortunately they know what you're for, too. Not much. There's really no end to the impositions, the slights. That's over now.

He knew the answer, though there was no question asked. It was the answer to everything. The sun continued its indolent march across the wall, the clock slowed down, and he wrung out the last piquant drops of his former, childish life there in the bed. His mother would call up to him soon, then roust him like a bum sleeping in the park soon after that, but for the first time in his life, he wouldn't care. Everything had changed.

He was going to get money.

No, that was the wrong term. "Get." He would have money. There's the rub. He could see it was the pursuit of it that was the unmaking of the man. If you grubbed after it they'd fleece it from you. Money was the bait. You had to pass by the trap. Hard to do. Until you wake up one morning and understand it.

His father was forever getting money. One scheme after another. He started out like everyone else, with this stock here and that bond there. Hell, there was even money in a can in the pantry. What the old fool never realized that it was the selling that was worth something when he was buying. And when it didn't pan out, they'd buy it back from him to sell it to him again later. He took his own life over it. But really, didn't they take it from him? He just acknowledged that plain fact with a pistol in the garage.

He knew he'd best them all, because he'd love it for its own sake. He didn't want things. He'd never want things. If you want things, you try to get money to get them and then they'd have you again. You're a mouse that can't stay in your hole, and the cat outside it tries to look sleepy and disinterested. He knows you want things.

He just wanted the money. He would sit on a big pile of it and do nothing. Everyone would come to him and tell him what they'd do for a bit of it. That would be their undoing. They'd ask for his counsel, although it was worthless. They'd want to be his friend though it was pointless. The money would make him the sun they would orbit, still lonely and distant in the cold reaches of space. The promise of a little warmth, an orbit one ring closer, and he'd have them.

But you couldn't try. It had to show up, like barnacles accreting on a slow-moving ship. What to do?

He went down to the kitchen table. His mother was a bit bewildered to find him awake and dressed without a fight. She placed the food in front of him, and nattered about the sunshine on a long summer's day.

" Mom, give me four quarters."

"What for?"

"Doesn't matter. Don't bother about it. Just give them to me."

She was confused by the strange, calm look on his face. He must want a treat, but was ashamed to ask for it. She gave him the coins. That boy always let money slip right through his fingers, just like . . .

No, she couldn't think it. She turned her back to him and busied herself in the sink. An errant drop of salty water added itself to the thin scrim of soap. When she turned around, he was gone.

He walked the half-mile to Congress Street. He stood on the edge of the curb for a long moment, reflexively fingering the coins in his pocket. He looked across the street, and through the shop window he saw his classmate working his way around the pharmacy with a dust cloth. There was a tray right there in front of him, full of quarters and more, ready to pop open with the touch of a button.

But the money wasn't there for his friend. His friend wanted things, so he worked all summer to get money. But when the leaves turned and the first school bus roared up the street, he'd have nothing anyway. He'd give the coins he earned back to the owner for the trinkets he coveted and then promptly forgot.

Just then a car pulled up. A woman got out and fussed over herself. Straightening the line of her hose, smoothing a wrinkle over the curve of her hip, pulling out a little circular mirror from her bag and making that odd, pointless motion at the corner of her mouth with her pinkie, removing an imaginary smear of lipstick. She was beautiful, and he was invisible to her.

A policeman turned the corner down the block. He was making his way slowly down the streets, resolutely reminding his neighbors they'd lingered too long in some shop with a ten-dollar ticket. He'd turn the little thumb-lever on each meter, as if there might be a coin stuck in there he could release, and so save some honest but harried shopper the sinking feeling of finding a rectangle under the windshield wiper. How many times had he done it to no effect? That was never it. And yet he kept doing it, over and over, like chanting in some dead language in an abandoned church. He did it to make himself feel better, because in his heart he was ashamed of what he was doing.

The woman stood at the meter, holding too many things. She looked at her watch. She looked down the row and saw the policeman. She held in her hand a dollar bill.

"I'll give you three quarters for that," he said.

The Same River

I'VE WALKED UP this street so many times now. I can't really remember how many times.

You can never put your foot in the same river twice.

Heh. High School teachers. What would they know about it? Their feet never get wet. It sure feels like the same river when your boot's full of it again.

I can tick my finger through the slats on Atkin's fence, and feel the easy rhythm of it in my bones. I can anticipate which will be out of alignment enough to break the pulse of it. I know it. I painted it once for summer money.

I know exactly when to shrug past the light pole and dodge around each mailbox, and the precise amount I've got to raise my foot to clear the curb, without looking. The neighbor's dogs don't even bark at me. They know me like I know them. I'm not the same as when I left, but I smell the same, I guess.

I like the way the rocker at 27 goes back and forth in the breeze. I could always look out the window and see how much breeze there was before I went out. There's never a person in the chair, so it's more useful. Funny, that.

The lawn's gone to seed. Mom never would push that fiendish little mower with the curling blades going swish swish inches in front of your feet, and the finely shorn blades of grass cascading onto your shoes. It always made her peevish, to be so close to danger and to be expected to be disinterested in it. I could tell her a bit about that now.

Dad had to go and die on her. His back was too strong for his heart, she said. She says I got all his heart. She got the mower.

She's alone, but not lonely, she wrote to me, because she has him and me in her heart always. She says death and the grave is nothing. Nothing but your troubles ends at the edge of the hole in the ground, she'd said while we each threw in a handful of gravel, eight summers ago. Mom cries when she reads novels but not in a boneyard.

I always put my right foot on the first step. It's the spot already worn from dad's boot. I wear away at the spot in his place now. Someday I'll wear it clean through and I won't know what to do, because that hole will be dearer to me than a religion, but how do you keep a hole? There's Dad -- gone again in another hole.

The door has that heavy oval glass in it. I used to run my finger around the bevel, to feel the clean edge and marvel at the perfection of the curve of it. Dad said I'd be a man when I could reach all the way around without tiptoes. I showed him I could. He let me mow the lawn.

The paint's peeling on the jamb, except around the doorbell, where it's worn all away. There must be a lesson in that, but I don't really care what it is. I can see straight through the house from the stoop, the rooms opening one into another in a line. Mom's in the kitchen, at the end of the parade. Her hair hangs in her face like it always did when she was working. A wisp on either side of her eyes. She brushes it back with the side of her hand, and her head turns, and she sees me there in the glass.

She stares at me a good long while. She leans on her hand on the tabletop, like I've seen her do a thousand times a thousand times when the kitchen gets too hot.

Maybe I should have written. Maybe I shouldn't have worn the uniform. Maybe she doesn't know me right away. Maybe I'm different now.

8755722R0